Bodge
Plants a Seed

A retelling of
The Parable of the Sower

Written and Illustrated by
Simon Smith

Zonderkidz

Zonder**kidz**®

The children's group of Zondervan

www.zonderkidz.com

Bodge Plants a Seed
Copyright © 2004 by Simon Smith
Illustrations copyright © 2004 by Simon Smith

First published in the United Kingdom in 2001 by HarperCollins*Publishers*
First published in the United States in 2004 by Zondervan

Requests for information should be addressed to:
Zonderkidz, Grand Rapids, Michigan 49530

Library of Congress Cataloging-in-Publication Data

Smith, Simon, 1966–
    Bodge plants a seed : a retelling of the parable of the sower / written and illustrated by
    Simon Smith.-- 1st.
       p. cm. -- (Clay pot parables)
    Summary: Jimmy carefully plants his seed and tends to it while his friends are careless.
    ISBN 0-310-70662-9 (Hardcover)
    1. Sower (Parable)--Juvenile literature. [1. Sower (Parable) 2. Parables.] I. Title. II. Series.
BT378.S7S65 2004
226.8'09505--dc22

                                       2003018668

Editor: Gwen Ellis
Design direction: Michelle Lenger

Printed in China
04 05 06 07 /HK/4 3 2 1

For Ellie and Ed

Down at the bottom of a long-forgotten garden, four mice were walking.

Each of the mice had a seed to plant.

"I'll plant my seed later," said Stumpy.
"First I want to play!"

Stumpy dropped his seed
on the path, and he
didn't even notice.

He was too busy playing
chasing games with the squirrels.

"I'll plant my seed now," said Big Al.

But he didn't choose a good place.
The ground was dry and rocky.
It was a shady spot.
Big Al's seed didn't grow.

"I'll plant my seed now," said Jimmy.

He chose a good place.
The soil was damp and soft.
It was a sunny spot.

The sun came out,
and the rain fell.

And Jimmy's seed grew . . . and grew . . .

. . . and grew into a little green plant.

But then the rain didn't fall.
And Jimmy's plant
stopped growing.

It went all brown
and droopy
at the edges.

Then the insects came
and chewed holes
in all its leaves.

And then weeds grew up all around.
And Jimmy's plant died.

"I'll plant my seed now," said Bodge.

He chose a good place.
The soil was damp and soft.
It was a sunny spot.

The sun came out,
and the rain fell.

And Bodge's seed grew . . . and grew . . .

. . . and grew into a little green plant.

But then the rain didn't fall.
And so Bodge gently watered
his plant. And it grew an extra leaf.

Then the insects came to chew holes in all the leaves.

But Bodge scared them away.

Weeds began to grow up all around.
Bodge pulled them up and threw them away.

And Bodge's plant grew . . . and grew . . .
and grew into a big, tall plant.

Bodge took care of
his plant.
It got just enough rain . . .

And just enough sun . . .

And a big stick
to climb.

And Bodge's plant
grew a big, beautiful
flower at the top.

Stumpy, Big Al, and Jimmy looked up at Bodge's plant.

"I wish my seed had grown up so tall," said Big Al.

"I wish my seed had grown up so well," said Stumpy.

"I wish my seed had grown up so beautiful," said Jimmy.

So Bodge gave them each a seed
from his great big plant.

"Maybe you'll give your seed a little
more care this time," he said.

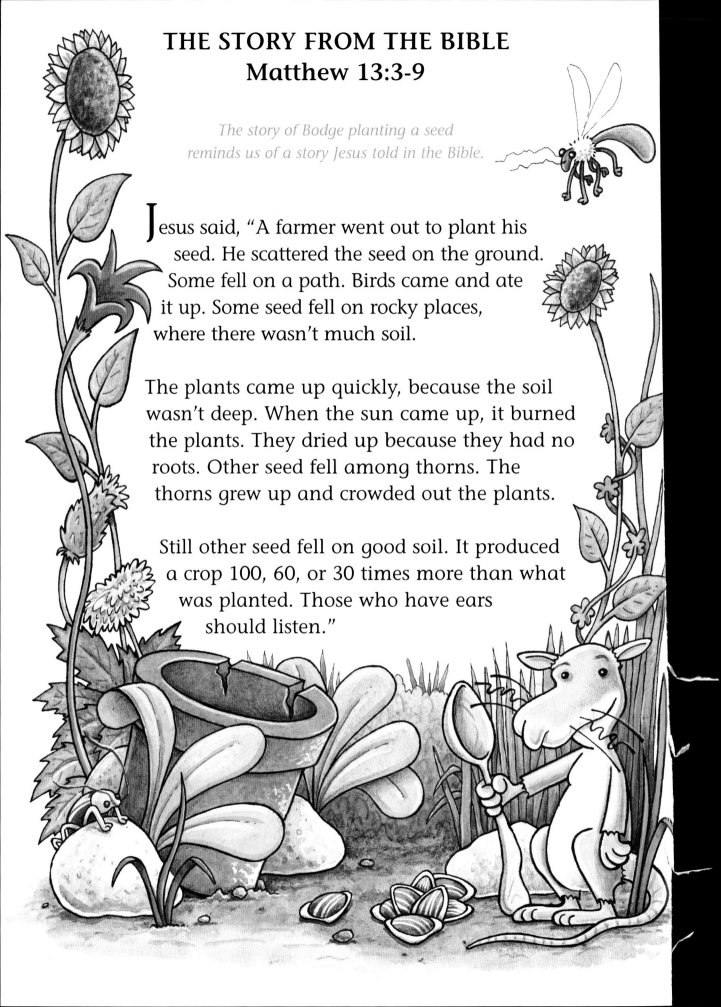

THE STORY FROM THE BIBLE
Matthew 13:3-9

*The story of Bodge planting a seed
reminds us of a story Jesus told in the Bible.*

Jesus said, "A farmer went out to plant his seed. He scattered the seed on the ground. Some fell on a path. Birds came and ate it up. Some seed fell on rocky places, where there wasn't much soil.

The plants came up quickly, because the soil wasn't deep. When the sun came up, it burned the plants. They dried up because they had no roots. Other seed fell among thorns. The thorns grew up and crowded out the plants.

Still other seed fell on good soil. It produced a crop 100, 60, or 30 times more than what was planted. Those who have ears should listen."